The Cat and the Fiddle

Cathy Farr

Moon Dreaming...
where adventures happen

This book is published by BITE Publishing, Cardiff.

A copy of this book is available at
the National Library of Wales and the British Library.

ISBN 978 099 285 09 44

The book and cover pictures are copyright of Mike Terry
(www.thepaintbrush.co.uk)

Cover design and typesetting by Ritchie Craven
(ritchiecraven@gmail.com)

Printed in Wales, UK by Gomer Press
(gomerprinting.co.uk)

'Hey, diddle, diddle,
the cat and the fiddle,
the cow jumped over the moon;
the little dog laughed to see such fun,
and the dish ran away with the spoon.'

Mother Goose

The Cat and the Fiddle

All was quiet at Number 27, Ambrose Avenue... well, quiet except for the click of Grandma's knitting needles in the next room. And quiet except for the sound of Randolf ('Yes, with an 'f,'' as Grandma always reminds the vet's receptionist) snoring loudly; at least, at the moment, he was snoring (Grandma was experimenting with some new food that really wasn't agreeing with his tummy).

'If that dog farts again this evening he's sleeping in the garden!' Dad had threatened earlier that evening while waving the latest copy of *Cars Monthly* under his nose. But *Corrie* was on the TV and Grandma, being quite deaf on occasion, had the volume turned up so she didn't seem to hear him.

Now, with the television volume back to normal downstairs, Max lay in bed listening to Randolf's grumbling snores and wondered what Grandma really would say, if Dad made Randolf sleep in the garden.

It was good to have something to think about, and to listen to. It took Max's attention away from the wardrobe door... Oh no! There, he'd thought about it again!

He tried to think about Randolf snoring... Grandma knitting... But his eyes were drawn towards the dark wardrobe that loomed in the corner of the bedroom he shared with his twin sister, Evi. Even in the darkness he knew that the door of the wardrobe was very slightly open – it always was – leaving just enough room for something... anything... to hide behind.

Max looked away. If he looked back now he knew something would be looking back at him through the crack in that door... or he would catch sight of a hand: gnarled, crooked fingers with blood-red nails scraping across the battered sky-blue paintwork, nails sharpened and ready to–

The bedroom door opened and as soft light flooded into the room Max heard a voice whisper, 'You still awake, Max?'

'Er, yeah,' answered Max. He suddenly felt very foolish – monsters... in wardrobes... at his age? Nah!

Max's Dad took a step into the room.

'Everything OK? Do you need a drink... or a wee?'

'Er, no thanks,' Max mumbled.

'OK then, son, try to get to sleep. See you in the morning.'

Dad turned to go, adding, 'Hope the bed bugs don't bite!' He said that every night.

Max sat up. 'Er, Dad.'

His father's hand was on the handle of the bedroom door.

'Yes, son.'

'Can you close the wardrobe?'

Dad took three strides to the other side of the room and gently pushed the door closed. 'Do you want me to leave the landing light on?' he asked, moving to the window where he pushed the curtain aside with the back of his hand. 'You know what I used to do at your age when I couldn't get to sleep?' Moonlight shone onto the bed against the opposite wall where Max's twin sister, Evi, was sound asleep. Max hauled himself up onto one elbow; he had the distinct impression his father was about to share a precious secret.

'What?'

'I used to look up at the moon and imagine I was having an adventure. And before I knew it, I'd be having the best dreams right through 'til morning.'

Max studied the bright orb in the night sky.

'But what adventures did you think about?' he asked, not being able to imagine anything nice – the wardrobe door had swung open again.

'Oh, the usual,' shrugged Dad. 'Saving pretty maidens from fire-breathing dragons, fighting a wicked, child-eating giant... my favourite was the werewolf – '

'Well, that's not going to help him to get to sleep now, is it?'

Mum had appeared at the doorway. Hands on her hips, Max could see she was still in her work uniform. She worked the late shift at Shop-u-Like, the local supermarket: she hated it, Max knew, but she'd taken the job after a big row with Dad about something called a mortgage. 'He's bad enough with the dark as it is!' his mother continued. 'Come on, Russ, leave him to get some sleep and stop filling his head with monsters.'

She was now at Max's bed, tucking the duvet up under his chin. 'Night, night, darling,' she whispered and stroked his cheek with the tips of her fingers. They were still cold from her walk home but Max didn't mind. She gently kissed him on the forehead then picked up Evi's teddy, Norman, who, as usual, had fallen out of her bed. Dad straightened the curtain and followed Mum to the door.

'Happy moon dreaming,' he whispered over his shoulder.

The door clicked shut and Max lay in the dark listening to his sister's steady, sleep-filled breathing. To avoid catching sight of the open wardrobe, he turned to face the window, leant out of bed and pulled the curtain open again.

'*Hmm, moon dreaming.*'

Outside the moon beamed down over the town. It had rained earlier and the soaked roofs shone in silver light.

Moon dreaming... But what on earth should he think about?

A movement outside caught his eye. There, on the corner of that roof over there... just behind the chimney. It was... it was Randolf!

Max partly fell, partly jumped out of bed and pressed his nose against the window unable to believe what he was seeing. What on earth was Randolf doing on that roof? The little dog had trouble with the stairs in their house because he had eaten too many doughnuts; Grandma had been told about the doughnuts during Randolf's last visit to the vet.

'Oh, but he loves them,' she had argued.

'And I love pies, Mrs Crumpton,' the vet had said while peeling a rubber glove from his hand. 'But I don't eat them every day. *And* I run ten miles four times a week!'

Max squinted into the darkness. He was sure he could see Randolf's tail wagging... and... was he? ... Yes, he was looking right at Max... He was beckoning Max with his paw!

Max jumped back into bed, shut his eyes, counted to five and... funny, he could feel cool air on his face... and his feet were standing on something cold, damp and very hard. Max opened his eyes... and nearly toppled off the roof!

He shut his eyes again quickly.

A bored voice right next to him spoke. 'It's OK as long as you don't look down.'

Max opened one eye. All he saw – apart from the moon, and the stars in the sky, and the slate of the roof he was now standing on, and the garden – a very long way down! Other than those things, all he saw was Randolf, Grandma's elderly and slightly tubby terrier (Grandma always insisted proudly that he was a West Highland terrier, but Max's friend Henry Porter's mum had one and it certainly didn't have long, droopy ears and a ginger patch over its right eye like Randolf).

This time Max shut his eyes tight.

'I was hoping you'd come. I've been snoring for ages, you know, to keep you awake.' The voice paused then started again, slightly peeved. 'No Evi then?'

'She's still in bed,' said Max. He had decided he was dreaming and that any minute now he would just drift into another dream about school chairs eating Mrs Bartlett (a bit of a favourite daydream, if Max was being honest – Mrs Bartlett's spelling tests were much harder than Mr James's last year… *triumphant*… with a ph, not an f – who knew!).

Beside Max something tutted.

'Great! Well I suppose one's better than none. Look I've got a job on and I need your help. Come on.' A pause. Max was still concentrating on the insides of his eyelids. 'Didn't think to bring your slippers then,' said Randolf, sounding not unlike Max's mother the last time he went to stay with Aunty Audrey in Devon. Max liked Devon – nice ice cream… and sand; but he wasn't that keen on Aunty Audrey. She was a bit too fussy about sand. Max heard Randolf's voice again, this time it was a bit further away.

'Well, mind the moss.'

'Oh. Why?' Max asked. His eyes were

open now. True, he was still on the roof but he decided to just go along with it until he woke up. 'Will my feet get dirty?'

The overly round ginger and white terrier looked at the boy then peered down at the huge gap between where they were standing and the garden below. 'Something like that, yeah.'

Randolf set off at a trot along the ridge of the roof. He jumped down onto the ancient outside loo, landed on a water collection barrel and was standing on the lawn before he next looked around. Max was still on the roof.

'Well, come on! I haven't got all night!'

'But I don't think –,' Max started.

Randolf put his paws on his hips.

'Great! A friend's in need; you go for help and what do you get? Some wimpy bozo that can't even climb off a roof!' Randolf turned away in disgust and trotted off towards a gate in the wall at the bottom of the garden. Something in a hedge hissed.

He ignored it. 'Don't worry, kid. I'll sort this out myself. You go back to bed.' He skidded to a halt and spun round. 'And no helping y'self to my doughnuts, you hear me! I'll be needing them to rebuild my strength after this!'

Alone on the roof, Max was trying very hard not to feel scared; he was failing. The roof around him was turning white with fuzzy frost crystals and he was starting to feel decidedly chilly. If this was a dream, he thought he would really appreciate waking up in his nice warm bed any time now.

A long way below, a gate creaked open then bumped shut.

'No, wait!' he called; Randolf – or dream Randolf – may be the only way he could get out of… whatever he was in.

The gate did not creak back open.

'Oh dear,' Max moaned. 'I really hope this isn't going to be one of those falling dreams where I wake up just after

I've stepped off the edge of something very high – I really hate those dreams!'

Muttering 'This is only a dream, this is only a dream,' over and over, Max crept, slipped and tumbled down the roof. He almost followed the same route as Randolf; only the little dog had made it look far easier, despite his rotund frame. After what felt like an hour, as was often the case in dreams, Max felt damp grass under his bare feet.

'Randolf!' he whispered. No answer. 'Randolf!'

Trying to call out in a whisper was not nearly as easy as it sounded. Max was beginning to get frightened. He had no idea where he was, or how to get home. He was just about to really shout when he noticed a pair of wellies right in the middle of the lawn. Now, Max knew that if this really was a dream the wellies would do something like walk towards him, or start dancing, or something horrid that he decided not to think about… he held his breath and waited. Nothing. Max wondered if the wellies were waiting for him to do something. He took a step towards them. Still nothing. Max took another step. In the end Max gingerly approached the wellies – they stayed stubbornly still. His feet were now very cold and wet, too, from the frosty grass. He slipped his soggy left foot into the left welly and got ready for something to happen… when nothing happened he slipped his right foot into the other well. All around him remained quiet and unchanged. The wellies were certainly a bit big, but they were also fleecy-lined and once on, Max decided, they were not coming off anytime soon!

Feeling considerably more comfortable, if not still very nervous, Max trudged off towards the gate. Now his feet were nice and warm he started to feel very slightly braver. He decided that if he didn't catch up with Randolf he would try to make his way home – although he was also hoping he'd wake up before he had to set off as he wasn't entirely sure how he was going to get back into the house even if he did find it: in the evening when Mum got in from work Dad had a habit of locking every single door and window in the house.

Max pushed open the gate, wondering just how Randolf had got out of their house; it was certainly quite some time since the tubby little terrier's tummy had fitted through the dog flap.

'Well, nice of you to join me!'

Max's heart nearly stopped in fright. Randolf was leaning against a wall.

'You found the boots then. Good. Hope they fit.' Randolf padded away down the moon-lit lane, talking as he walked – his voice getting fainter as his tail got more distant. 'Mrs Strumley'll be planting her asparagus crowns tomorrow so we'll have to get them back to her when we've finished.'

Max got the impression he was meant to follow. The returning of Mrs Strumley's wellies started to bother him; with no idea as to where they were, he had no clue how they would get the wellies back to her – whoever Mrs Strumley was!

'Are we going home?' Max panted hopefully when he caught up. Running in oversized wellies, he was discovering, was not as easy as you'd think. In the end he found that an exaggerated stomp seemed to work best.

'Little Pippin Farm,' said Randolf, making no effort to slow down or make any allowances for Max's lack of speed. Max stopped dead.

'Little Pippin Farm!' he gasped. 'In Oakbrook? But… but that's miles away. Literally miles! We went strawberry picking there last year with Dad. We took Grandma, too. It took so long she made Dad stop twice. She said it was to avoid an accident.' Max frowned at the memory, briefly forgetting the issue in hand. 'Although, I didn't think Dad's driving was that bad.'

To his amazement, when Max next looked up, right in front of him was a huge sign bearing the words *Welcome to Little Pippin Farm* in big green lettering. There was also the familiar picture of a badly drawn strawberry that looked more like a bright red potato, and the words, 'Pick your own – strawberries are far more fun than noses!' Max liked that sign. His Dad had explained it to Evi and him. They had laughed for ages – in fact, after their visit last year it had become a bit of a joke at home, although Mum didn't seem to find it funny anymore.

'Right, Max. Keep your eyes open… and, more importantly, your ears.' Randolf, who had been left at home for last year's visit, strode straight into the farmyard past a second sign saying 'No Dogs'.

'But who… what are we looking for?' asked Max, with a certain dread as to the answer the terrier might give him. Suddenly the memory of his Dad's moon dreaming ideas came to mind – dragons, giants, werewolves… The hairs on the back of Max's neck prickled. The farm yard was spookily quiet. There had been cows in the field when he'd come before in the daytime, and chickens all over the yard, and a massive red tractor. Now everything was very quiet, dark and… squelch!

Max's left leg suddenly felt cold. He looked down. Even in the darkness he could see that one pyjama leg was a lot darker than the other one, and a lot wetter. Max reached down.

'*No!*' hissed Randolf.

But it was too late. Max's fingers found the sticky, almost fresh manure that had just splashed up his legs as he stomped around the yard.

'I sincerely hope you aren't going to roll in it, too!' said Randolf, looking deeply unimpressed. He turned away and looked across the farmyard, his nose in the air, sniffing as he searched.

'Randolf, what are you looking for?' Max insisted, dragging his hand over a hay bale and trying not to breathe-in too deeply. 'If this is a dream, I really think I need to wake up now. This stuff honks!' He kept as close as he could to Randolf who was sniffing his way across the dark yard towards some even darker farm buildings. Max tried not to stomp; Randolf ignored him.

At the first of the buildings the little dog pressed his back up against the rusty metal wall. He surveyed the scene by flicking his eyes from side to side before he dropped back on all fours and crept along the wall with his tummy even closer to the ground than was usual. Feeling more nervous by the second, Max reluctantly followed. His eyes were drawn to every very dark patch of darkness and the hairs

on his neck refused to lie flat. Suddenly there was a clattering from somewhere behind them. Randolf, still hugging the wall, disappeared around the corner of the building, and with absolutely no wish to be left behind Max picked up the pace. He rounded the corner of the metal-clad building at a trot. Crump! Max ran straight into Randolf.

'Oof! Oh, oh, s-sorry,' stammered Max. 'W-what are you doing?'

Randolf was gingerly sniffing a metal dish of white liquid.

'Hmm,' he said eventually. 'This isn't a good sign.' He lapped at the contents of the dish and wrinkled his nose. 'This milk's on the turn.'

It was Max's turn to put his hands on his hips. 'Well, if we've come all this way for a snack, Randolf,' said Max, suddenly feeling brave – sour milk! *Really?* 'I'm sure Grandma would have given you some back at home – to go with your doughnut!'

Despite his fear of dark, creepy places, Max was feeling slightly peeved that this dream, or whatever it was, was so far rather chilly and a teeny bit boring. It was time for an explanation. Max sat down abruptly on an upturned bucket.

'I'm not going anywhere else until you tell me why we're here and what we're looking for. And if it's a hungry hedgehog, I can tell you now, you'll have to fight me for the doughnuts when we get ho–'

Randolf was holding up his paw for quiet – the other paw was pointing across the yard. Max looked in the direction of the pointing paw. Lying flat out, right under a massive tractor that Max knew to be red, was a black shape. Randolf took off at a gallop.

'No, no, no. Please, don't let it be him. No. Oh, I'm too late.'

Max followed although the overly large wellies were proving more of a hindrance in the rushing department.

'Go back and get that bucket,' ordered Randolf without losing speed. Max did a u-turn, grabbed the pail with a clatter and lumbered back; the metal handle of the bucket clanked and rattled with every step Max took. Randolf was standing over the black shape now. It was a cat. Randolf nudged the cat with his nose: it burped loudly, rolled onto its back and hiccupped. Max caught sight of a violin propped up against one of the wheels of the tractor. One of the strings was broken.

'Oh, Alvin, what have you done?' wailed Randolf.

The cat opened one eye. 'It's too late, old friend. You're too late.'

'But...,' Randolf's ears drooped. He plonked his bottom down, just missing another cow pat and put his chin on his paws. Max returned the bucket to its previous upturned position and resumed his seat. Alvin hiccupped again.

'She's gone. I couldn't compete. On the third verse... I broke a string!' he wailed. 'It was a fair fight, I suppose. The best cat won... it's not whether you win or lose, it's how you play... better to have fought and lost tha–'

'The bucket, Max,' said Randolf, back on all four paws. 'Go fill it with water, there's a good lad.'

Max was surprised by Randolf's suddenly tender tone. He looked past the huge tractor wheels.

'Where's the tap?'

'Over there, behind the chicken shed,' said Randolf without taking his eyes away from Alvin who was now singing badly. He still had hiccups.

Fortunately, the moonlight shining right across the chicken run made Max's hunt for the tap fairly straightforward and he placed the bucket on some rotten and very soggy boards that seemed to have been placed there for just such a job and turned on the tap. Then he turned it off again... and listened. He could hear a small and very frightened voice.

'No, no, just let me go. I did what you asked. You won, didn't you? She's yours now. Leave us alone!'

There was a terrible hissing sound, followed by a loud 'Eek!'

Max abandoned the bucket and crept around to the front of the chicken shed. He held his breath and peered around the corner with as little of his head as he dared to reveal.

There, in the chicken run, bathed in moonlight, was a big tabby cat, and under

one of his front
paws was the
tail of a not
terribly big
rat. The cat
was staring
intently at the rat attached to the tail; the
rat seemed to be trying very hard to put
some distance between it and that stare.

'But he's still here,' hissed the tabby.
'And she will not love me if she knows this.'

'I know,' whimpered the rat. 'But the
deal was that if I arranged for you to win
the game, you would leave me and my
family alone. I gnawed the string, he lost,
you won. Now just – let – me – go!' The rat
was straining now, trying to pull its tail
away from its captor. But the cat planted a
second paw on the tail.

'No, rat.' The cat put its face right up
to the rat's ears. The rat closed its bright
beady eyes. Max was sure it was also
holding its breath. 'The deal was, if I

remember correctly, that he would lose and meet with a nasty accident on the main road. But he is still here and my mistress's cider barrel is running low.'

As he talked, the tabby's tail slowly flicked from side to side. The rat was now stone still. Max was also stone still. He was listening as intently as the rat; were they talking about the same cat that Randolf had just found? Cider would certainly explain those hiccups... and the really bad singing (Max's mum was partial to a quick chorus of 'Let It Go', from *Frozen*, when she'd had a few glasses of wine – always loud and very awful).

'Now, this is what you are going to do, rat,' purred the cat, his voice suddenly full of a charm that made Max's skin break out in goose bumps. 'You, or your children, I don't care who, will set a trap that gets him under the wheels of anything passing this farm by the end of this night. You will then show me, and my beautiful new lady, the results of your efforts – preferably smeeeeared.' He lengthened the last word as if to stress his desire. 'If you fail this simple task my beautiful new lady and I will feast on your family every day until only you are left... then I will eat you.'

A bored voice behind him made Max nearly jump out of his skin. 'If you're waiting for rain we could be a while.' In the chicken run the tabby looked up.

'What was that?'

'W-what?' answered the rat, still cowering.

'A voice. Someone spoke... over there. Not the mistress, not my beautiful new lady; another one, unfamiliar.'

Max could see the tabby arching his neck to investigate; his tail was up apart from the tip which curled round towards his head – it looked just like a question mark. Behind him, Randolf took a breath; Max knew the terrier was going to speak again. Without thinking Max clamped his hand over Randolf's muzzle. A loud hiss and a terrible yowling made Max look back towards the chicken run; the rat was nowhere to be seen. The cat, however, was skittering out of the yard like its own tail was on fire.

'Run!' yelled Max heading for the nearest very dark corner of the very dark farm yard, as far away from the chicken shed as he could see; he didn't like the dark but he liked the sound of that tabby cat even less.

From somewhere else a woman's voice called out, 'Hyde! Dinner. Hy-yde!'

There followed another hiss from out of the gloom, then the sound of cutlery banging against metal.

'Hyde! Din-dins. Come on, Booffies.'

Bang, bang, bang!

'Hyde-y, Darling.'

Max was sure he could hear a tiny voice muttering, 'Ooh, ow... if she does that much more, I swear I'll... '

The woman spoke again.

'Oh, there you are. Hello, handsome. Have you been playing with the yard cats again?' Max heard the sound of a door closing and peace returned to the farm yard; even the appalling singing and the muttering had stopped.

Max stepped out of the shadows. Randolf wasn't standing in the shadows. He was standing in the middle of the yard, paws on his hips, with a look on his face that could freeze blood.

'I'll just go and get that water,' said Max.

Max was holding Alvin at arm's length.

'Are you sure?' he asked Randolf for the second time.

'Yep!' said Randolf in a voice that would curdle milk.

'But Grandma told me that cats don't like water. Don't they melt or something?'

'Melt, no,' said Randolf. 'Sober up, yes. Now put him in!'

Max carefully lowered the snoring Alvin towards the water. By the time the cat's second claw touched the icy surface he was awake and scratching his way up Max's arm: by the time Max felt any pain the cat was on the roof of the tractor behind him.

'W-w-w-what did you do th-that f-for?' stammered the cat. 'I hate w-w-water!.. R-R-R-Randolf, i-is that y-you?'

'I can't believe he's shivering like that,' said Max. 'He didn't even get wet!'

Randolf looked up at the cat and said very quietly out of the side of his mouth, 'It's a stammer, Max, and he's very conscious of it. Would've mentioned it but someone had their hand clamped around my nose!'

'Oh,' was all Max could think of to say.

'Look, Alvin, we're here to help. Come on,' said Randolf gently, gesturing with his paw. 'Come back down. Come on. If you promise not to have anything else to drink, I promise my friend here won't give you a dunking. Just come on down and tell us what happened. Where's Lady…. And what on earth happened to your fiddle?'

On the roof of the tractor, Alvin slumped.

'N-no idea… and n-n-no idea,' he wailed. 'Hyde ch-challenged m-m-m-me to a-a fiddle d-d-d-duel. M-m-m-my string b-b-broke. I l-lost e-e-everyth-th-thing.'

Alvin began to wail.

'But he cheated', said Max, brightly.

'What!' said Randolf and Alvin together.

'I heard him, Hyde, talking to the rat.' Max knew how random this sounded but hey, in dreams animals talk all the time – don't they? 'The rat said something about gnawing a string so that you'd lose.' Max was careful to avoid any mention of the bit about Alvin being smeared over the road by a passing car.

The cat sat up, stood unsteadily, then even more unsteadily, climbed and slid down the cab of the tractor; the last bit, over the wheel, was more of a fall. Both Max and Randolf stepped forward to help but Alvin jumped to his feet with only a brief stagger.

'I'm alright! I'm fine' he insisted, without stammering. 'Right, boy, tell me exactly what you heard.'

When Max had finished telling them

about the conversation he had overheard in the chicken run Alvin sat for a moment then got up. Randolf jumped to his feet but the black cat turned away with a flick of his tail.

'It's OK, Randolf. There are some things a cat needs a bit of privacy for.'

Randolf looked sceptical. 'As long as it doesn't involve cider!'

'Well, it is the result of drinking it!' said the cat, over his shoulder.

'Why isn't he stammering?' asked Max as soon as Alvin disappeared into a bush.

'He only does it when he's stressed. He's great when he's singing… or fighting,' answered Randolf, with a note of admiration.

'So, tell me again,' said Randolf, stroking his chin with his paw. 'You thought you were playing for the dish of milk… but Hyde tricked you into giving up Lady – the one and only love of your life, never to be parted: been together since you were rescued from that awful place over at Thornton and brought here to live with Lady. You two... the farm cats – plenty of milk... blah, blah.'

'D-d-d-don't,' wailed Alvin. He had been calm up to the point he told them how Hyde had challenged him to a fiddling duel the previous night. Alvin had, he told Randolf and Max, been telling Lady about the pleasure of drinking milk fresh from the cows. Apparently he had just been saying how it was best still warm and creamy, and how it was the milk he loved best in the world when Hyde had turned up. With cobwebs dangling from his whiskers and a coating of dust from the long-forgotten, old, dry corn and barley that had fallen behind the grain bins in the store, it was obvious that he'd been terrorising the farm rats (Alvin didn't really mind them;

they liked his music, he'd told Randolf and Max).

'He s-s-suggested the duel and s-s-said if I won I c-could keep the th-thing I l-l-loved b-b-best in the w-w-world,' stammered Alvin. 'I assumed he m-m-meant the d-d-dish of m-m-milk, s-s-so I agreed.'

'But he didn't,' said Randolf flatly.

'N-no,' wailed Alvin. 'The r-r-rats b-b-brought cider. They said there wasn't any m-m-milk. It w-w-was only when my st-st-string broke... he s-s-said I'd l-l-lost Lady. He dragged her a-a-away...'

'Where is she now?' asked Max. Alvin was stammering so much that Max was having trouble following the story because he was concentrating on not finishing Alvin's words for him.

Alvin shrugged and pointed vaguely past the tractor's huge hydraulic boom and loading bucket (Max's Dad had explained all about the parts of the tractor when they'd finished picking the strawberries last year).

'They went th-th-that w-w-way. I'd had t-t-too much cider. C-c-couldn't chase... c-c-c-c-... ooohhhh!' He flopped onto the yard and began to yowl.

'Ahem!' A little voice in the dark shadows under the tractor cleared its throat.

Alvin jumped up. 'Lady! You've c-c-come back!'

'Er, no,' admitted the voice. A rat poked its nose out from behind the tractor wheel.

Alvin hissed. Suddenly he was on all fours; his back arched. The hairs down his spine were standing on end. It struck Max that at that moment Alvin did actually look quite scary. The rat's nose disappeared. Alvin stopped hissing. He waited, staring at the place where the rat's nose had been. Randolf took a step forward, holding out his paw in an attempt to stop the cat from pouncing if the rat reappeared.

'Er, hello,' Randolf said to the shadow of the tractor wheel. 'You still there? Look, he doesn't mean any harm... He's just a bit, er... tired and emotional. He... he'll be fine now.'

Max noted that Randolf's other paw was tucked behind his back – his claws were crossed. Alvin's back was still arched and the hackles along his spine were still standing on end but he was only mouthing a hiss now. He still looked scary though. Randolf tried again.

'Er, hi, there.' He took one more step towards the tractor wheel. 'Look, I promise he won't hurt you. I, er, I'll hold on to his tail.'

'Looks pretty mean to me!' squeaked a little voice from the blackness.

'Well, he's just had a bit of bad news and, er, he's not taking it well,' said Randolf. 'I, um, don't suppose you, er, know anything about it? Do you?'

High in the sky, a small, puffy cloud

had drifted across the moon sending the yard into total darkness. A feeling crept over Max… a distinct feeling that they were being watched – like a thousand eyes were studying their every movement, waiting to pounce. His goose bumps came back.

Suddenly the little cloud drifted on its way. The yard, once more, was bathed in bright moon light… and on every ledge, self, roof and fence post, Max could see pairs of tiny, bright beady eyes – every one looking directly at them… well, Alvin actually. 'Whoa!' breathed Max.

'KXSSSSSSSSSS!' hissed Alvin.

'I see you brought some friends,' said Randolf.

'Just give me the one who broke my fiddle string,' Alvin demanded. 'I'll rip him apart limb from limb... but don't worry, I'll sing while I'm doing it!'

'You're not helping, you know,' muttered Randolf, hardly opening his mouth.

Suddenly Max's world changed. It was darker than pitch and he wasn't sitting on the up-turned bucket any more... Randolf was nowhere to be seen... Alvin was silent... and the tiny eyes had stopped twinkling. Max moved. All around him rustled. Straw? He was lying in what felt distinctly like a bed of straw – a lovely warm bed of straw. The smell was not a million miles away from the smell of his cow poo-covered pyjama leg – although he was getting a bit more used to that now – and Alvin's yowling had been replaced by a rhythmic munching sound. Max reached up into the darkness. His fingers found something soft and warm. He inched his hand up a little more and groped what felt like soft, fat fingers. He gave one a gentle squeeze. The rhythmic munching stopped. Max, more curious now than scared, continued his exploration; convinced that he was fondling a soft glove (although the reason why the fingers were slightly stiffer than you'd expect in an empty glove, he chose not to think too much about; but whatever it was didn't feel unpleasant). He slid his own fingers further up and touched a big warm balloon. He gave that a gently squeeze.

'You haven't had much practice at this sort of thing, have you?' said a kind voice.

Max nearly jumped out of his skin yet again. In a flash he withdrew his hand and, again, tried very hard not to breathe. Just maybe the thing attached to the voice would assume he'd gone – or it would go and he'd find himself somewhere else in his dream.

'I know you're still there, you know,' said the voice. 'Just be careful I don't tread on you.'

A big eye was looking right at him. The eye blinked slowly.

'Dragon!' thought Max, all his worst fears bumping into each other in his imagination. *'Please let me wake up. I know this is only a dream! WAKE UP!'*

But Max didn't wake up. The eye blinked again. Huge legs either side of Max shifted, kicking the straw around as they moved. Max was frozen in terror. The dragon was moving around to blow flames all over him, he knew it; it was going to barbecue and eat him where he lay. And he hadn't told his Mum and Dad how much he loved them recently... or Evi!

'Now keep still and I'll try not to stand on you,' said the dragon.

'You OK in there, Betty?' asked a slightly more distant voice.

'Oh yes, Glenda,' answered the dragon standing over Max. 'Well, if you call being cooped-up in here all day and night "OK", I suppose. I do seem to have a

41

bit of company though.'

'Not those rats again? Drunk and lost, I'm guessing?' guessed Glenda. 'Or is it that blinking cat? Y' know, the new one... Hood, Clyde... something like that. Tried to use my udders as a scratching post yesterday. Stopped when I gave 'im a swift hoofing, mind.'

The eye glanced at Max again. Somewhere else in... wherever he was... something gave a soft, 'Moooo.'

'No, it's a boy,' said the... er, dragon? Max wasn't so sure now – Betty and Glenda didn't sound very dragon-like names. Certainly the absence of fire was making him think again... and the mooing... and the smell of manure. Then the munching sound started again – all around him.

'Um,' said Max, addressing the dark-shape above him. The munching stopped again. 'Are you a cow?'

'Well, I would have thought the udders were a bit of a giveaway,' said the cow above him, with the slightest hint of surprise. 'And I managed to work out you were a boy without any clues at all!'

Max got onto all fours and crawled towards the cow's voice.

'If you want to get out I'd go the other way – towards the back end,' said the cow helpfully. 'But watch where you put your hands; I haven't quite got to grips with the drain yet.'

'Drain? What's that for?' asked Max as he shuffled backwards, hoping that the cow wasn't going to tread on him, or give him a quick 'hoofing'.

'To catch the poo, dear,' answered the cow, her voice suddenly sad. 'Haven't been in a field for days. It's the new foreman's idea. He's come from a huge place north of Nordale. They keep the milkers in all the time there. Reckons they save on feed, get more milk and don't need acres of grass. He's persuaded Emily to try it here. Needless to say, we hate it.'

'Haven't felt the sun on me back or grass under me feet for days now,' said another cow in the next stall. 'And I'm not happy about it neither.'

'But I trod in a poo outside in the yard... just now,' said Max.

'Yes,' said Glenda, nodding towards the far end of the parlour. 'Hetty, over there, made a break for it this afternoon. Half an hour it took them to get her back in. I think the muck was a bit of a protest vote. Hey, Hetty, a protest vote?' She raised her voice slightly. 'Good on you, Girl!'

'Oh,' said Max, not really knowing what else to say. He remembered their visit last year. They'd watched the cows grazing in the field while they had a picnic – well, a MacDonald's actually. And Dad had let them have fries after he'd made them promise not to tell Mum. Grandma had had a MacFlurry so she promised too.

'Well, I don't reckon my milk's any better,' sighed Betty. 'My heart's just not in it.

I noticed Alvin left his yesterday, too. Emily always puts a saucer of milk out for the farm cats... although that Hyde drinks it more often than not!'

'Hyde, that's it,' said Glenda with a nod. 'He's trouble that one. You can't give a cat the luxuries of home-living and then expect it to be a farm cat, too. They just don't understand the rules. The fighting's been terrible, hasn't it, Betty?'

'Oh, yes, poor Alvin' said Betty. 'And I haven't heard him playing his fiddle all day. No wonder my milk's not right.'

'Well, I know why Alvin's not playing his fiddle,' brightened Max. 'Hyde challenged him to a fiddling duel and cheated. Alvin lost. Hyde tricked Alvin into giving up Lady and now no-one knows where Lady is!'

'Um,' interrupted a frightened voice, 'I'm here.' And out from the stall opposite, like a little ghost, stepped a beautiful, smoke-grey cat.

Max was sitting on another up-turned pail, this time in the middle of the milking parlour. The cows had all stopped eating. They were listening intently while, between them, Max and Lady put together the true story of what had happened earlier that night when Alvin lost the fiddling duel. Lady's black-lined eyes had narrowed when Max explained what Hyde wanted the rat to do.

'But I just don't understand it,' said Lady, shaking her head. 'That rat, Stephen, has never been any trouble. He and his family... they never take more grain than they need and they leave our saucer of milk alone. They even stopped eating the hens' eggs once we agreed to share the odd bit of chicken Emily gives us as a treat.' Lady turned to Max and with a sad look added, 'She's the farmer. Her husband, Fred, he's the one who rescued us... I mean Alvin and me. He died three years ago.'

'But it's that Hyde who's been a bit of a problem for you, hasn't he, dear?' said Betty carefully.

Lady looked down at the floor. 'Well, it hasn't been ideal since he arrived,' she said equally carefully. 'He can be quite good fun, don't get me wrong. But... well, he's just such a bad influence; he even introduced the rats to cider.'

'Cider?' said Max, not really knowing what cider was, but guessing from Lady's tone that it wasn't good for rats... or cats.

'Fred used to make it. There's an apple orchard in the bottom field. Emily's just kept up the tradition,' Betty answered helpfully. 'The local restaurant buys most of it, I think.'

Lady nodded.

'He got Alvin to try some too.' She wrinkled her pretty little grey nose. 'I didn't like it. And Alvin and I... we never seem to have any time on our own anymore. I liked it when it was just the two of us. But Hyde's always turning up, betting he can do something better than Alvin. The fiddling duel was just another bet. And Alvin being Alvin,' she pressed her lips together and looked skywards then carried on. 'He just can't resist taking up the challenge, and the cider seems to make him worse. He's just not used to it – he drinks milk... he *likes* milk. The other day Hyde bet that he would be able to catch a robin before Alvin. Alvin agreed to compete but only if Hyde promised to let the bird go when the winner was announced. Stephen was there then, too, acting as referee.

Alvin won. But when Steven agreed that Hyde had lost, Hyde killed the robin and chased Stephen. It was awful!'

'So why does Alvin go along with it?' asked Max, although he had a good idea he knew the answer. There was someone just like that in his class at school – Toby Wright. At the beginning of term Toby had bet Max that he could kick a football over the school fence into the garden opposite the teachers' car park – if Toby did it he'd get the Snickers bar that Max's mother had put in his packed lunch that day. Max said he couldn't because they weren't supposed to be playing in the car park anyway. But Toby did. Then he took Max's lunch box, ate the Snickers and threw the rest of Max's packed lunch over the fence too. Max had tried very hard not to cry, although it had been a close-run thing. After that he kept well clear of Toby Wright at lunch-time.

'Because Hyde's cunning,' answered Lady, her voice breaking with sadness. 'He knows Alvin'll do things to try to impress me, silly old thing. Hyde knew that Alvin wouldn't back down if I was there. I tried to stop him, but... ooh, and now look what's happened.' A tear plopped into the straw at her feet.

'But if Stephen's your friend, can't he help you?' Max remembered Hyde's threat to Stephen's family. He wondered how Randolf was getting on with Alvin... if they'd managed to talk to the rats... or if Alvin had eaten Stephen before he'd had chance to explain his side of things.

'I think Stephen's too frightened... if you'd seen what Hyde did to that robin.' Lady shuddered and closed her eyes as if to blot out the memory.

'Yes,' agreed Max, not allowing his imagination to even get going. 'Hyde threatened Stephen's family, too!'

'So, does Hyde know where you are

now, dear,' Betty asked Lady, her voice calm and kind.

Glenda raised her head to try to look out of the window. 'I certainly heard Emily calling him before you crept in here. Banging away with that spoon, poor thing,' she said, her voice full of disapproval. 'So you came in here to sleep in the straw – lovely and warm, isn't it?... Though it's not grass, of course... or a field... ' Glenda's voice tailed off.

Out in the yard the sound of a woman's voice brought an instant hush over the little group in the parlour.

'Alright, puss, if you weally, weally want to go back out to play. The cat flap's open so Hyde can come in for a nap when ever he wants. Mummy'll keep a nice comfy spot on her bed just for Hyde-y.'

'Is that Emily?' asked Max. Grandma certainly never spoke to Randolf like that!

'Yes,' said Betty. 'Honestly, it's pathetic. She wasn't like this before.

He's got her wrapped right around his little finger – paw!' She corrected. 'What with that blessed cat and the new herdsman; I know, with Fred gone it must be difficult but I just don't know what's happening to this farm. They'll be rid of the strawberry picking before we know what's happening!'

'They can't do that!' Max objected. 'I really liked strawberry picking – I ate loads!'

'Well, *we* liked living in a field, with grass. *We* ate loads... and look at us now cooped up in here all day and night,' said Betty waspishly. 'All good things ending seems to be a bit of a theme around here at the moment!'

A loud sob drew everyone's attention back to Lady.

'And if we don't stop Hyde and Stephen, the best thing that ever happened to me will come to an end tonight as well!'

Max sat and thought for a moment. Lady cried quietly. The cows shuffled in the awkward silence.

'You didn't say if Hyde knew where you were,' said Max after quite some time. 'Does he?'

'He probably thinks I'm still in the rusty feed bin behind the old milking parlour,' she said. 'That's where he took me after he'd won.' She dipped her front paws to indicate speech marks when she said "won". 'I don't know what he was planning but when he heard Alvin singing in the yard a little while ago he said some very bad words, dragged me into the feed bin and slammed the lid shut! Said he had something unexpected to sort out... We all know what that is now, don't we!' She started sobbing again. 'He told me to stay and wait for him. He kept calling me his "beautiful new lady" – but I'm not his. Alvin and I belong together. I don't know what I'll do if anything bad happens to Alvin.'

'How did you get out of the feed bin?' asked Max.

'The back is really rusty where the gutter's leaked onto it for years. I just gave it a bit of a push and it fell apart.'

Outside there was a sudden yowl and the clang of metal on metal.

'Hmm, I think Hyde may have just discovered your escape, Lady,' said Max in a hurried whisper. 'Betty, Glenda, Girls,' he addressed the whole herd briefly. 'I've got to find Randolf. Keep Lady hidden here. Randolf'll know what to do, I promise!'

As this was a dream, Max really thought he would suddenly be transported back to Randolf, who, he hoped would be with Alvin, and if Stephen was there too, that would be even better. But Max didn't go anywhere. Disappointed and a little confused, Max padded back out into the yard, ducking into every shadow until he was almost back at the hen house. The moon was tucked behind another cloud and the only light was coming from an upstairs window of the farmhouse. The light went off. Max, once again, was in complete darkness. Feeling his way along the wall of yet another building – wooden this time – it was starting to cross his mind that he couldn't hear any of the sounds he was expecting to hear: no sound of Randolf being right, Alvin being heart-broken, or rats being... well, what ever rats did. (Not having a lot of experience of rats, Max was not at all sure what they did when they weren't being terrorized by a large tabby cat that had hold of their tails).

What Max could hear was an odd, muffled sound – a very annoyed muffled sound.

He rounded the corner of the shed just as the moon revealed itself again. Suddenly there was movement and sound everywhere – scurrying, squeaking, scampering; tails disappearing as black shapes squeezed under other buildings, then... stillness and silence.

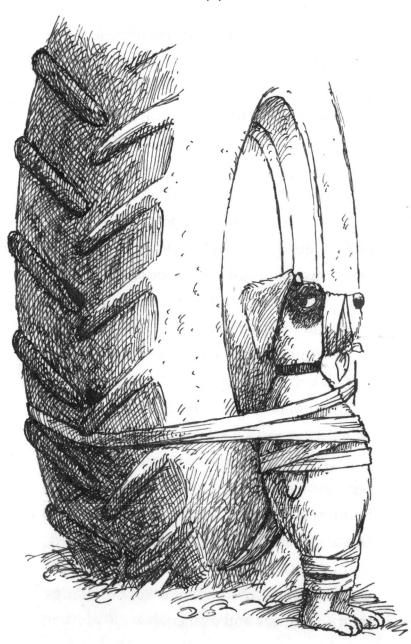

Startled by the sudden, albeit short-lived, commotion, Max inched across the yard in the hope of finding something familiar... and preferably friendly. He squinted towards the chicken shed. The massive tractor seemed to loom out of the shadowy darkness and right up against one of its huge rear wheels Max could see a pale shape. The very annoyed muffled sound started again – it was coming from the pale shape. Max crept forward. The annoyed, muffled sound got louder and the shape got clearer. Max gasped.

'Randolf!'

'Hmmm mmm mfff!' said Randolf. 'Mmm!

'What happened?' Max asked undoing the bandages tied around Randolf's muzzle. Questions dived around Max's brain and spilled out of his mouth.

'Where'sAlvin?Ithoughtyouweregoing totalktotherats?DidyoufindStephen?He'sthe oneHydedidthedealwith.' Max stopped to breathe. He opened his mouth to start talking again but Randolf beat him to it.

'Shut up! Shut up! Shut up!'

Max shut up.

'It's bad enough that I've just been overpowered by a bunch of rats and a tabby-cat and tied to a tractor. But I absolutely draw the line at being talked to death by a small boy in his Scooby-Doo pyjamas covered in cow poo!' Randolf looked Max up and down. 'Did you have Scooby-Doo pyjamas on earlier?'

Max looked down. 'Er, yes... no... I don't know.'

'Surely you know what pyjamas you put on when you go to bed?' asked Randolf sounding genuinely surprised; Max knew that Randolf would have had his paws on his hips again if he hadn't still been tied to the tractor.

'Er, ... not really,' answered Max. 'Mum, or sometimes Dad, puts them on my bed ready for when I've cleaned my teeth. If I have a bath Mum puts them on the radiator – Dad forgets. She irons them, too.'

'And what exactly did your last slave die of?' Randolf asked dryly. 'Exhaustion!'

For a second Max toyed with not untying the rest of the bandages that bound the little dog to the tractor; he was silently surprised that there were enough to go around Randolf's expansive tummy.

'Come on then, Scooby, what're you waiting for?' demanded Randolf. 'Undo these ties so we can go get those pesky rats!' He burst out laughing.

'Why are you laughing?' Max asked, still toying with leaving Randolf where he was.

'Pesky!' chuckled Randolf. 'The rats.' He raised his eyebrows, still chuckling. Max's face remained blank. 'You haven't seen the film, have you, kid?'

'What film?' asked Max.

'Scooby-Doo,' answered Randolf, his smile fading.

'No,' said Max. He looked down at the large, grinning dog on the front of his pyjama top. 'Dad got me these for my birthday last month. Keeps saying "rooby-dooby-doo" every time I put them on... What does pesky mean?'

'Oh, the irony,' muttered Randolf. 'Just untie me, Max, there's a good boy.'

Randolf recounted what had happened while Max untied the bandages.

'Where did these come from?' Max asked; he certainly wasn't aware of any specific first aid skills rodents may have had.

'Tractor cab,' said Randolf, nodding upwards. 'It's unlocked. The keys are in there, too! They just went in and came back with rolls of the stuff. Must have raided the medical box. The foreman'll be livid in the morning. Probably'll blame kids.'

Max was quietly impressed by the knots – they were really difficult to undo.

All, apparently, had been going well at first. Randolf had persuaded a few of the rats to come out into the open and Alvin had, thankfully, not eaten any of them. Stephen had introduced himself (Randolf was interested to hear from Max that it was Stephen who had chewed Alvin's fiddle strings, as Stephen has failed to mention this). Stephen then had gone on to tell Randolf about the very complicated family tree of the rats at the farm; an awful lot of the rats appeared to be related to an awful lot of the rats but Randolf skipped over that bit leaving Max rather confused, although he decided there were more important things still unanswered, like where was Alvin?... and, had they seen Hyde?

The answer to the first question, it turned out, was tied up in the answer to the second: Randolf explained that Stephen had just got to the bit about the duel when

Hyde had jumped down from the roof of the chicken shed, licking his lips and smelling of tuna. He was all charm at first; apologised to Alvin for cheating and asked if Alvin had found Lady. But when Alvin had told him that he hadn't seen Lady and accused Hyde of keeping her captive somewhere, things had begun to get ugly.

'Hyde kept insisting that Alvin knew where she was and, of course,' shrugged Randolf. 'Alvin had no clue. Alvin then got cross and told Hyde that if he didn't tell us where Lady was, things really would get ugly.' Randolf wound one of the bandages into a roll as he talked. 'Hyde just laughed.'

'What happened,' asked Max.

'Things got ugly,' replied Randolf.

Max groaned. 'Oh, no.'

'You can say that again,' said Randolf, throwing Max a warning glare just in case he did. 'Hyde shouted, "Get them!" There was a blur, a lot of squeaking, and suddenly I was tied to this tractor here and Alvin was bound-up and bundled into some sort of trolley... with wheels. I think the farmer uses it to move the milk churns around, or hay or something? Anyway, the rats've taken Alvin. They went that way.' Randolf pointed towards the main gates. As if carefully timed, a car whizzed past on the road outside.

'Did they say what they were going to do?' asked Max.

Randolf shook his head and put his paws on his hips.

'No, but I heard Hyde muttering some horrible threats regarding Stephen's children when they were dragging Alvin away. He's got a really nasty laugh, you know... quite evil, even for a cat!'

'Randolf, is that you?' asked Lady, slinking between Betty's legs. 'Oh, I'm so glad you've come. Has your friend told you what happened? Have you... do you know where Alvin is?'

Max noticed that Randolf was trying very hard not to catch Lady's eye. He kicked at some straw and seemed to find a pile of crusty manure terribly interesting.

'Er, yer, he's fine, Lady. Just keeping out of the way until we can get this thing with Hyde sorted out.'

Lady purred for the first time.

'I knew it would be alright,' she smiled. 'Probably sleeping off that cider. Did you tell him I'm safe, Max? That I managed to get away from Hyde?'

Max looked at Randolf who didn't look back.

'Um, not in so many words,' Max answered. 'But I think we need to deal with Hyde first... and the rats.'

Lady stopped purring.

'Yes, of course. So, Randolf, what's the plan? I hope you're going to get rid of Hyde once and for all!'

Several of the cows mooed their agreement.

Randolf plonked his bottom down onto a patch of bare concrete and sighed.

In an effort not to catch Lady's eye either, Max looked around the parlour. Just beyond Glenda's stall he caught sight of the lifting boom of another tractor. Two big wheels were lying either side of boom... then Max remembered. Of course! His father had explained that the wheels span around pushing hay and straw away from the middle of the parlour and back towards the cows so that they could carry on eating while they were being milked – which at the time Max and Evi had both thought was terribly clever.

Randolf shifted awkwardly. 'The thing is, Lady, ...'

At that moment Max had an idea.

'The thing is, Lady,' he interrupted, and for once Randolf looked relieved. Max continued. 'We're going to lure Hyde into a trap. Randolf and I just need to go and check something first... '

Max was on another roof. This time Randolf had joined him in his dream-jump. Max breathed a sigh of relief; he hadn't quite formulated the plan he was about to announce and hoped that Lady wouldn't be too alarmed by their sudden disappearance.

Below, he could see a neat little front garden that he guessed belonged to the farmhouse. Max also saw a movement in the far corner of the little garden.

'Look! There,' said Randolf. He had obviously seen the same thing. 'That's the trolley that they hauled Alvin away in. Can you see? Look, there's Hyde… and the rats! Come on!'

Randolf was just about to head down the roof when Max grabbed hold of his tail. Randolf stopped.

'I am going to ignore what you just did, boy, as we are in crisis. BUT, if you ever grab hold of my tail… or my nose again, I may not be responsible for my actions.'

Max let go of Randolf's tail.

'What exactly did you have in mind?' asked Randolf, his tone surprisingly patient.

'Well, if that's the trolley, where's Alvin?' said Max.

'Which is why we need to get down there… to look!' said Randolf, less patiently.

'But if we go down and he isn't there, they'll see you, know you escaped and that we're looking for Alvin. They might take him somewhere we can *never* find him,' said Max reasonably. 'Let's just stay here a minute and see what's going on… by the way, can you drive?'

Max knew this was a very strange thing to ask a dog but as he'd spent most of the night talking to an array of animals his idea of 'strange' had shifted somewhat over the past few hours.

'Yeah,' said Randolf carefully. He threw Max a guilty glance. 'Was that a trick question? Your Dad's car. I only borrowed it once – goodness me, it's fast! Bella at Number 4 was sooo impressed!'

'Bella? Mr Powell's poodle?' asked Max.

'Er, yeah,' said Randolf, looking decidedly shifty. 'Ooh, look! There's one of the rats. Look, there... ooh, what's Hyde doing?' Randolf was leaning forward so much Max was convinced his hairy little friend was going to fall off the roof; but after Randolf's recent threat Max was careful to keep his hands to himself.

Randolf leant a teeny bit further... unfortunately, a teeny bit too far.

'Ooooooh!' He oohed, running down the roof as fast as his little legs could carry him. 'Can't stoooop! ... Oooooof!'

Max sat down on the slippery roof and pushed himself forward. He slid; when he got to the edge he closed his eyes... and landed on something soft.

'Oooof! Ahhhh-cchew!' Max sneezed. He looked around. There was no sign of Randolf. Max felt sick; what if Randolf hadn't landed on the compost heap that had just broken his own fall? Then he spotted a tubby, white shape some distance away, creeping along the edge of the lawn under the line of a shaggy-looking Leylandia hedge. (He knew it was Leylandia because last year Dad had planted a whole line of them between their house and Mrs Peacock next door and she was really rude to Dad about them. Dad had said he didn't care because he didn't like Mrs Peacock anyway). At the sight of Randolf scampering along unhurt, a wave of relief washed over Max... followed immediately by the desire to shout, 'NOOOOOOO!' very loudly.

Randolf was moving straight towards Hyde, who was running towards Randolf. The rats and the trolley had disappeared again. Max blinked. Randolf seemed to be running in slow motion. Max shook his head and blinked again. Hyde was also running in slow motion. This dream was getting stranger by the second; although it didn't really matter how fast (or slow) they were both running; they would still crash into each other if Max didn't do something. But what?

Frantically, he looked around for something to throw, or break, to distract them. Nothing. He was in the tidiest garden in the world. Then he spotted a lawn mower tucked away in an almost empty wood store at the top of the garden. After two steps Max realised that Mrs Strumley's wellies were going to have to go. At this moment he needed speed not warm feet so he kicked off the heavy boots and pelted to the store. He grabbed the mower. It was just like the one at the tennis club where Mum cleaned on a Saturday morning. Max had got into really bad trouble last July because having managed to start it he mowed down the groundsman's tulips – all of them. Mum nearly got sacked and Max's weekly Haribo ration had been stopped for a month – it had been a hard summer!

With a strong heave on the cord the mower roared into life. Max pointed it in Hyde's direction, let go and ducked back into the shadows. The mower couldn't have been better aimed. Hyde skidded to a halt, turned tail and galloped back down the garden in the opposite direction – he was going at proper speed again – the mower trundled after him. Randolf looked around to see what the commotion was and ran straight into an over-hanging branch. The only thing that really surprised Max was that no-one from the farmhouse came out to see what all the noise was about – but that's dreams for you, he guessed.

Randolf was groaning and spitting out bits of green when Max caught up with him.

'I'm quite sure, *ptf,* there's a perfectly reasonable explanation for why, *p-ptfff,* a lawn mower has just passed me, *ptf,*' said Randolf, between spits.

'You were about to crash,' explained Max, 'into Hyde. It was the only thing

I could find.' He watched the lawn mower disappear into the darkness. 'Worked though!'

'Hmm,' hmmed Randolf. The sound of the mower stopped abruptly. 'I think we'd better go and see just how much havoc you've caused. Just be careful!' He set off on tip-toe. 'By the way, why did you ask me if I could drive?'

'Oh, it's just an idea I'm working on,' whispered Max.

'Oh, this is not good,' said Randolf, ducking back behind a little, low fence.

Max took a quick peak. The fence ran between the garden and the driveway – all the way down to the open gateway… and the road.

'Oh.' He too ducked back down. 'That wasn't meant to happen!'

'No, I suspect not,' said Randolf, wrinkling his nose. 'In fairness, the chance that rats would be able to operate a lawn mower was, in any body's book, a bit slim.'

Max peered over the fence again. The rats had somehow managed to stop the mower. Max had no idea what they were planning but he had a bad feeling it was going to involve Alvin, and probably not in a good way. Max crouched down again.

'Look, I think there's a way out of this. It's a bit of a long-shot but if we're going to help Lady and Alvin, I think this might be our only hope.'

Randolf put his hands on his hips. On the other side of the fence the mower roared into life again.

'OK, kid, try me.'

Randolf looked very strange in the cab of the tractor and Max was impressed that the little dog could reach the pedals, even if he was standing on tip-toe on his back legs to do it. Luckily the gap between the steering wheel and the seat was just wide enough for Randolf to squeeze through, although

Max hadn't said anything about that – neither had Randolf. Instead Max took a deep breath and patted Randolf on the shoulder.

'Right, you know what you're going to do now, don't you?' He jumped back down onto the floor trying to sound far more confident than he felt. The tractor cab suddenly looked very high up.

'Yes,' said Randolf patiently. 'You're going to distract Hyde by telling him you know where Lady is. You'll lead him into the cow parlour. In the meantime I'm going to go and scoop the mower into the bucket to get Alvin out of harm's way... in a manner of speaking.' He muttered the last bit under his breath. Max heard but decided to ignore what the little dog had just said.

Instead he said, 'Good. Once Hyde's in the parlour I'll knock him out with a bucket... or something... I'll find something... and tie him up with the bandages the rats used on you. When the milk lorry comes I'll hide him in the cab and he'll be gone from here before he wakes up.'

Max thought it was a good plan, and if Randolf had any doubts he wasn't sharing them.

Max looked up at Randolf and waited.

Randolf looked down at Max.

Max raised his eyebrows in what he hoped was an encouraging way.

'Oh!' said Randolf suddenly. 'You mean now!'

'Er, yep,' said Max. The tractor roared into life. 'I just hope we're not too late!'

It was only as the tractor pulled away did Max realise that Randolf couldn't really see past the bonnet of the huge machine. He was just about to shout when the little ginger and white terrier hopped up onto the seat and planted his front paws on the steering wheel; across his face was a huge grin.

'I really do hope this is only a dream,'
breathed Max and charged past the
trundling tractor, around the farmhouse
to the driveway where he skidded to a
halt and gasped.

The rats were
just launching

the mower off down
the gently sloping driveway and there in
the grass box was poor Alvin, bound and
gagged, and looking very, very unhappy
about it.

Hyde was at the top of the drive
prowling to and fro; tail flicking from side
to side, he was purring with pleasure and
waving at the mower.

Max had no other choice but to trust
Randolf – or his dream. He had to stick

with the plan otherwise he would risk losing Alvin and the farm would never be rid of Hyde.

'Ahem!' he coughed. 'Mr Hyde? I, er… sorry to disturb you… if you're busy?'

Hyde slowly looked around, still purring loudly.

'No, boy, you're not disturbing me. Why would you think that? I…,' he slunk up to Max and slid his body along Max's leg. 'I have all the time in the world, boy.'

The purring was quite deafening. Max could only just hear the mower; he couldn't hear the tractor at all and hoped that was a good thing. The mower was drifting off down the long drive. In the distance Max saw the headlights of another car flash past on the road. He tried his best to concentrate.

'Er, I… I've found a small grey cat… says she's a friend of yours.'

Hyde stopped slinking but carried on purring.

'My beautiful lady!'

Max shrugged as casually as he could.

'No idea. But she told me she's been looking for a handsome tabby who said he'd come back for her. Apparently she's been waiting hours. She's worried he's forgotten about her.' Max was trying not to gabble and failing. He could see that the mower was nearing the road. At last, from the other side of the farmhouse Max heard the gentle rumble of the tractor. He kept talking, a little louder now. 'You're... you're a tabby, so I was just wondering... I can take you to her... if you want? She's really missing you, you know. Gosh, she's a pretty cat.' He edged backwards towards the milking parlour as he talked, praying that the cat would follow. Hyde's purring had become positively enthusiastic; he was completely engrossed in Max's wonderful news.

'My beautiful lady, waiting for me? Where has she been?'

'I... er, ... she, she got cold waiting in the dark so she went into the milking parlour. Found a nice pile of straw. Said she's been keeping it warm for you,' Max lied. They were at the parlour door now. He hadn't had time to go back to Lady to tell her his plan. He was just hoping that she had hidden herself well enough away that they wouldn't be able to find her; Max still didn't know exactly how he was going to knock the tabby out.

Alarmed by their arrival, the cows mooed as Max led Hyde down the central walk-way, trying very hard to ignore the feeling of manure squidging between his now bare toes; although, on the plus side, it was warm. One of the cows kicked out but, sadly, missed Hyde completely.

'So, where is my beautiful lady?' purred Hyde. 'I cannot wait to be reunited with her. To take her to my special gift that my friends are currently preparing.'

'Oh, she's just up here.' Max pointed

towards the darkest corner in Betty's stall and prodded Betty hard in the bottom. She didn't move. 'She's been telling me how much she loves you, you know.' He prodded Betty again. The cow shifted her weight from one back leg to the other, munched once and looked around with one eyebrow raised. Max didn't prod her again. At that moment a scared voice spoke in the darkness.

'No! No! Max, you said you'd help. You said you were Alvin's friend. What are you doing bringing *him* back here!' Lady was shrieking by the time she'd finished. Hyde stopped dead. Too late, Betty lashed out. Hyde sprang back and scrambled up into the rafters.

'What is this?' he hissed. 'My beautiful lady does not sound pleased to see me, boy.'

'Erm,' said Max. He was trying desperately to get some sort of signal to Lady to let her know he was still on her side. He didn't know if Hyde could see him

(Grandma always said cats could see in the dark, and while he had no idea if it was true he didn't feel now was a good time to try to test the theory). 'I… I'm sure it's just a misunderstanding. Lady, Lady, it's fine. Come here. It's all fine.'

He stretched out his hand and was rewarded with a sharp scram. 'You lied, you lied!' hissed Lady, backing away towards the milking pumps. Even the cows started to join in, stamping their feet and kicking out. Their mooing was deafening. Suddenly Max realised he couldn't hear Lady anymore. He glanced down between Betty and Glenda's stalls. A limp grey form was lying right under the milking pump; one of the cows must have caught her with a hoof. Max looked up. Precariously balanced on the rails between the stalls, Hyde was carefully making his way to where Lady was lying.

With a shout, 'NO,' Max dived under the nearest stall and wriggled on his tummy until he could just reach Lady with his finger tips. She didn't move. Trying to avoid being trampled by the alarmed cow above him, Max managed to catch hold of Lady's leg and as gently as he could under the circumstances, he pulled her limp body toward him. Finally, with Lady held close to his chest Max stood up... and came face to face with Hyde. The angry tabby arched his back, spat and with all fangs and claws flexed, launched himself at Max. Max leapt sideways and batted Hyde out of the way with his free arm, right onto the forgotten milk dish. There was a loud, 'Ugh! What th-'. Sour milk splattered up the wall and the dish carrying Hyde skidded across the manure-coated floor and out through the parlour door disappearing into darkness. A tiny voice said, 'Oh, this really is too much!' Then all was quiet.

Hugging Lady as close as he dared, Max slipped and slid across the parlour to the tractor he'd spotted earlier. He was hoping that, like the other one, the keys would still be in the ignition... they weren't.

Max's heart was just about to sink as his plan disintegrated in front of his eyes when there was a huge bang and the side of the milking parlour crumpled like a sneezed-in hanky.

'YEEEEE-HAH!' yelled Randolf.

Rooted to the spot, Max watched the steadily advancing tractor demolishing the side of the milking parlour as it trundled forward. Inside the now partly outside parlour all the cows started mooing. At first Max thought they were frightened... until he heard Glenda call out, 'Come on girls, I smell grass!'

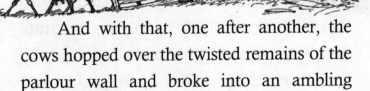

And with that, one after another, the cows hopped over the twisted remains of the parlour wall and broke into an ambling canter through the open gate into the nearest moonlit field. A glint of brightness also caught Max's eye: a silver dish was skipping through the same gateway and over the field, holding the hand of a… a spoon.

The tractor came to a juddering halt and the engine finally died.

'Think we're out of fuel over here,' called Randolf. It was fairly obvious from the sound of his voice that he was having a marvellous time. Max looked across the wreckage that was, until a very short time ago, a milking parlour, hoping the farmer would think the same thing when a terrible yowling made his stomach turn over.

'Oh – no – you - don't!' yelled what sounded distinctly like Alvin.

CRUMP!

'That's for cheating at the duel and trying to steal MY Lady!' shouted Alvin. Bang! 'And that's for bullying the rats into helping you!' Max peered around the door that Hyde had not long skittered through on the silver milk dish (the same one, Max was sure, he had just seen running away with the spoon) just in time to see Alvin swinging his fiddle high above his ears; Hyde was cowering with his paws over his head.

'No, no!' begged the trembling tabby.

Alvin was just about to bring the fiddle down on Hyde's head. 'And this is for that robin!' But as he swung the instrument forward Randolf grabbed it.

'I think you've made your point, Alv.'

Hyde, still on his belly, slid over to the terrier. 'Oh, thank you, good sir. Thank you. You saved me from this bully. Thank you.'

'Bully?' said Randolf, his paws taking their familiar position on his hips. 'Hm! I think the rats and that pretty little cat over there might just tell a different story!'

At the mention of the word 'rats', hundreds of gleaming pairs of eyes blinked from every shelf, ledge and piece of twisted metal in the yard and a voice squeaked, 'You can say that again!'

The limp cat in Max's arms stirred.

'Al-Alvin? Is that you? Wh-what happened?' Lady blinked and looked up into Max's face. 'Who are you?'

Before Max had chance to introduce himself for the second time that night Alvin leapt across the yard in two bounds.

'L-L-Lady, are y-y-you alright?'

'Bit of a headache,' Lady answered. She looked around and blinked her beautiful black-lined eyes again. 'What happened to the milking parlour?'

'It's a long story,' said Max. 'Alvin, how did you get off the mower?'

'That's a slightly shorter story,' grinned Alvin. 'But it's safe to say, I know who my friends are!'

One of the rats – Stephen, Max guessed – stepped out of the shadows holding up a bandage.

'As soon as Hyde disappeared we pulled the bows. Alvin never came near the road... although the mower's a bit of a wreck.'

Max looked back at the parlour again. 'It's not alone,' he murmured.

A little way off, Randolf was whispering something to Hyde. The tubby terrier shook his head, drew his paw very slowly across his throat and pointed to

Alvin, then to Lady, and then to the rats.
Hyde, looking very sheepish, nodded,
turned and walked away towards the
farmhouse without looking back. After a
few seconds they heard the distant bang of
the cat flap. Randolf clapped his paws
together.

'Right, well, Hyde has decided that
being a house-cat really appeals to him just
now, and if I'm not mistaken – and let's
face it, am I ever? – there's plenty of night
left, so I say, let's celebrate!'

'But what about the parlour?' asked
Max. 'I don't think anyone'll be celebrating
when they see that!'

Randolf put his paws on his hips and
surveyed his handy work. 'Oh, don't
worry about that, Max. These things have
a way of sorting themselves out... oh, and
by the way, did anyone else see the dish
and the spoon? Such a nice couple; it was
only a matter of time... I'm happy for
them...'

'Ma-ax... E-v-i, wakey-wakey,' called Mum.

Dragging himself out of sleep Max rubbed his eyes. He was in his lovely warm bed in his pale green bedroom with his slightly wonky picture of Spiderman blu-tacked above his bed. He looked over at Evi's bed, with her poster of *Frozen's* Princess Elsa on the wall: everything was just how it had been the evening before when his Dad had said good night and turned out the light.

Very carefully so that Evi wouldn't notice, Max ducked his nose under the covers and took a quick sniff.

'Er, Max! If you make the bedroom stink again I'm telling Mum!' shrieked his sister. 'MUM, Max has let one off again!'

'Get lost!' said Max, kicking the covers back. There had been no whiff of manure so he felt fairly safe to expose his pyjamas – they were indeed pristine, if a little wrinkled.

Downstairs, Dad was already sitting at the breakfast table. The radio was humming away in the background and Mum was just putting two pieces of bread in the toaster.

'Toast or cereal?' she asked. Waited and then asked again. 'Ma-ax, darling, wakey-wakey. Do you want toast?'

But Max wasn't listening. An announcement on the radio had caught his attention – he wasn't moving, thinking or breathing; just listening.

'And in the news this morning,' said the announcer, his voice suddenly grave. 'An out of control tractor caused thousands of pounds worth of damage at a farm in Oakbrook last night. Over to Sandra Gillingham who is at the scene. Sandra, what can you tell us?'

'Hello, Ash. Yes, the situation down here at Little Pippin Farm in Oakbrook this morning is like something out of a scene from *Transformers*. It seems that a tractor was left last night with the keys in the ignition and somehow started in the middle of the night. The vehicle, a Massey Ferguson, has not malfunctioned before but it was also left in gear, which appears to be where the problem lies. I'm joined now by farm owner, Emily Giles. Emily, have the police got any idea yet as to what happened?'

'Oh, no,' said Emily. 'The tractor was parked on the hill over there. I put it there myself. I've got a new cat, Hyde. He jumped into my lap while I was parking up last night. I must have got distracted and left the keys in. My lawn mower was found down by the road – that's rather badly damaged too.'

'And the cow shed?' Sandra Gillingham prompted.

'Milking parlour,' corrected Emily. 'Oh, that's a write off. Completely ruined... well, the twenty-four hour live-stock housing area is anyway. We managed to do the milking fine this morning. To be honest, the cows seems a lot happier to be back out in the fields and if the quality of their milk today is anything to go by, I don't think they'll be going back to live in the shed again.'

'So this accident could be a blessing?' asked Sandra.

'Weeell,' said Emily, with a note of caution in her voice. 'The quality of the milk had certainly dropped off since we've been trying this new system. Even the farm cats didn't seem so keen. I had my doubts from the start, but at least we can say we've had a go now.'

'So does this mean that the cows will go back to the fields?' asked Sandra.

'Oh, yes,' said Emily. 'Look at them. If I didn't know better, I'd say they were smiling!'

'MAX!'

Max jumped.

'For goodness sake, eat your toast!' Dad was loading the dishwasher as he spoke. 'You're making us late!' Max could never understand why his Dad bothered because Mum always took everything back out and re-loaded it again later. Dad carried on talking. 'We've got to drop something off for Grandma on the way to school this morning. Some wellies she borrowed from a friend of hers, apparently. Although why she can't just get her own pair, I have no idea!'

Max glanced in the direction his father's hand was vaguely waving. There, on the doormat, was a carrier bag containing a pair of exceptionally clean wellies.

'Oh', was all Max could think of to say.

That night Dad kissed Max on the cheek and pulled the covers under his son's chin.

'Nite, nite, Maxy, and happy moon dreaming.'

'Nite, Dad,' muttered Max.

Evi had gone to bed earlier as she was going on a school trip in the morning and

Mum had made Dad promise to get her into bed half an hour earlier than normal bedtime. Evi had complained bitterly but Max could see that she was already breathing the steady breath of someone fast asleep. As Dad pulled the bedroom door closed, the door of the wardrobe in the corner of the room creaked open. But Max didn't care. He could hear music. It sounded distinctly like the sound of a fiddle playing a jig.

Careful not to wake Evi, Max got up and pulled the curtain back.

Yes, it was definitely music; as he looked up into the sky he saw the very distinct shape of a cow jumping straight over the bright full moon… and a few streets across, right on the top of Mrs Strumley's roof was another outline – a tubby little terrier, laughing.

THE END